Whatever happened to the dinosaurs?

Written and illustrated by
Bernard Most

Harcourt Brace Jovanovich, Publishers

San Diego   New York   London

Whatever happened to the dinosaurs?

Also written and illustrated by Bernard Most
If the Dinosaurs Came Back
My Very Own Octopus
Dinosaur Cousins?
The Littlest Dinosaurs
The Cow That Went Oink
Pets in Trumpets

Requests for permission to make copies of any part of the work should be mailed to:
Permissions Department, Harcourt Brace Jovanovich, Publishers, 8th Floor,
Orlando, Florida 32887.

Library of Congress Cataloging in Publication Data
Most, Bernard
Whatever happened to the dinosaurs?
Summary: A humorous speculation on what really
happened to make the dinosaurs disappear.
[1. Dinosaurs — Fiction. 2. Humorous stories]
I. Title.
PZ7.M8544Wh   1984   [E]   84-3779
ISBN 0-15-295295-0
ISBN 0-15-295296-9 (pbk.)

Printed and bound by South China Printing Company, Hong Kong
C   D   E   F   G
E   F   G   (pbk.)

To every child (or grown-up)
who ever wondered about the dinosaurs.

We love to visit the library and read all about the dinosaurs.

But where did all the dinosaurs go?

They were so big and there were so many of them.

Why did they disappear?

Nobody knows. Even scientists are not sure.

The more we read about them, the more we wonder:

Whatever happened to the dinosaurs?

Did all the dinosaurs go
to another planet?
Maybe they're on
Jupiter or Mars.

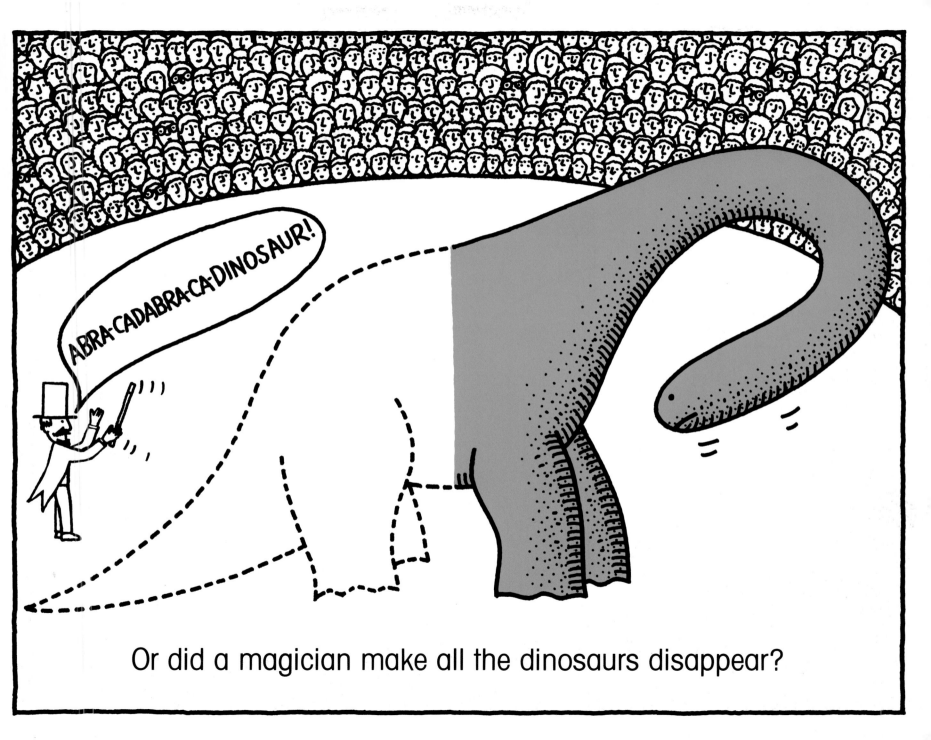

Or did a magician make all the dinosaurs disappear?

Maybe the dinosaurs are wearing disguises
and we just don't recognize them.

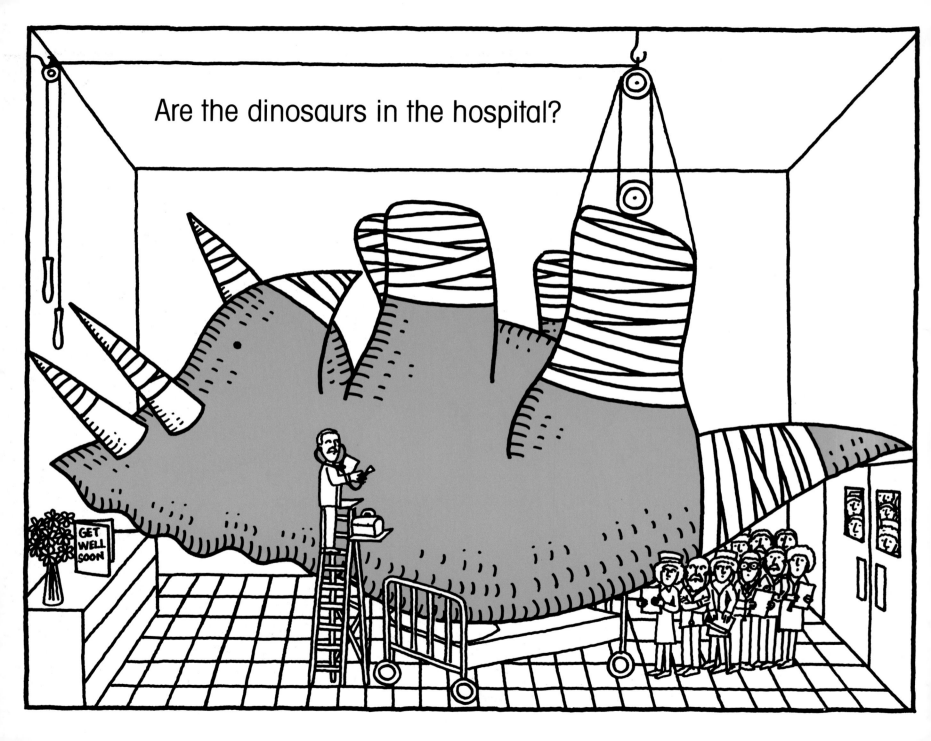

Or are they in jail?

Maybe the dinosaurs are lost
in the middle of the jungle.

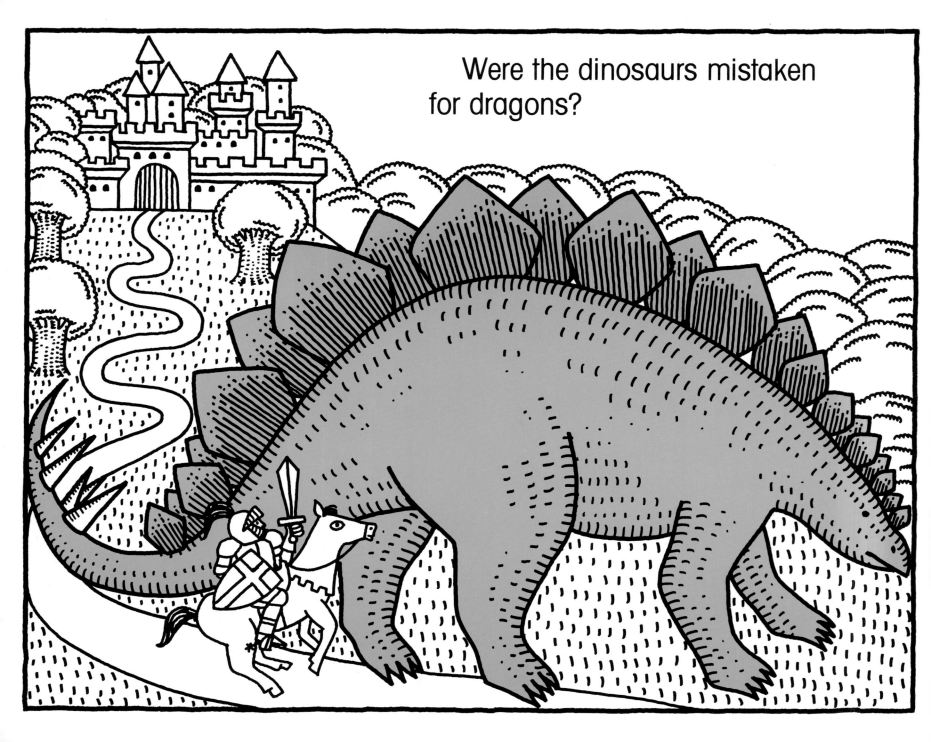

Were the dinosaurs mistaken for dragons?

Or did pirates steal them away?

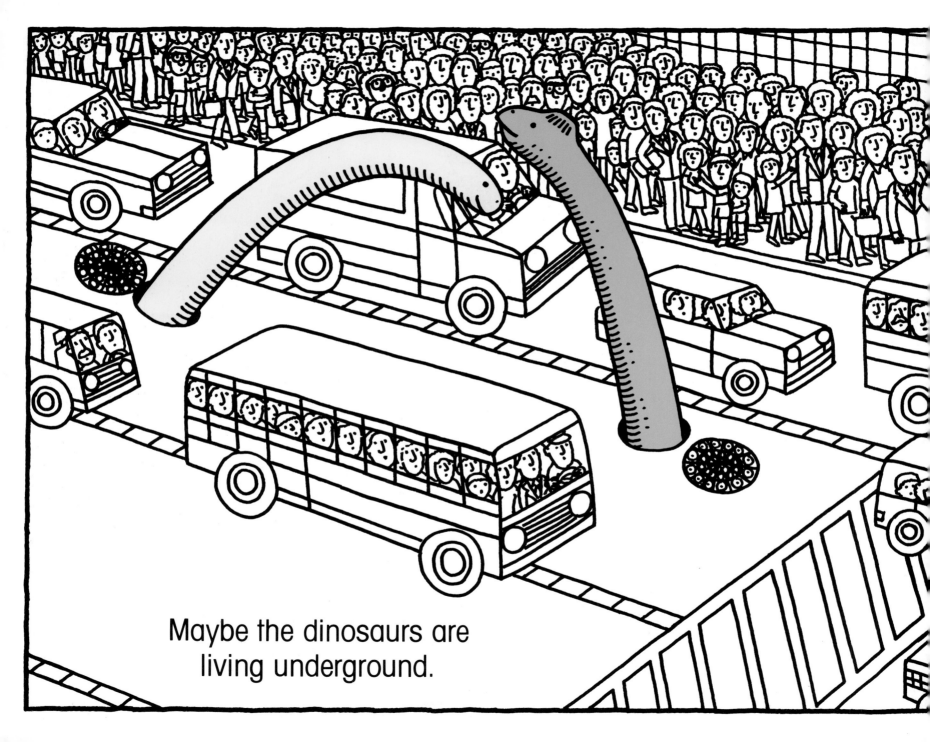

Maybe the dinosaurs are
living underground.

Did all the dinosaurs go on vacation?

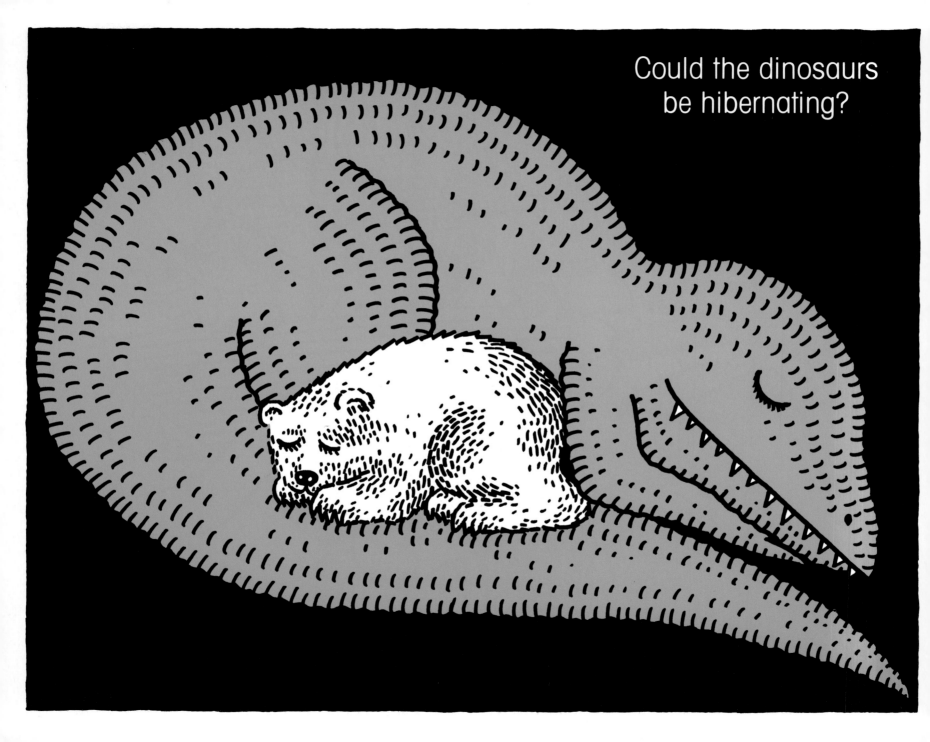

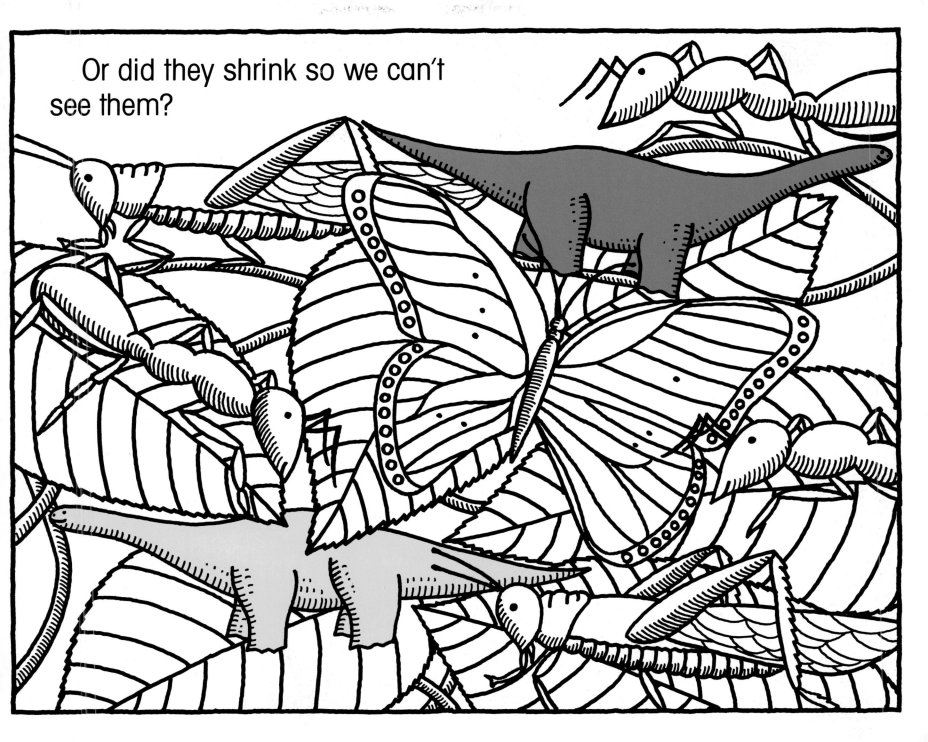

Or did they shrink so we can't see them?

Maybe the dinosaurs are at the North Pole.

Are the dinosaurs underwater?

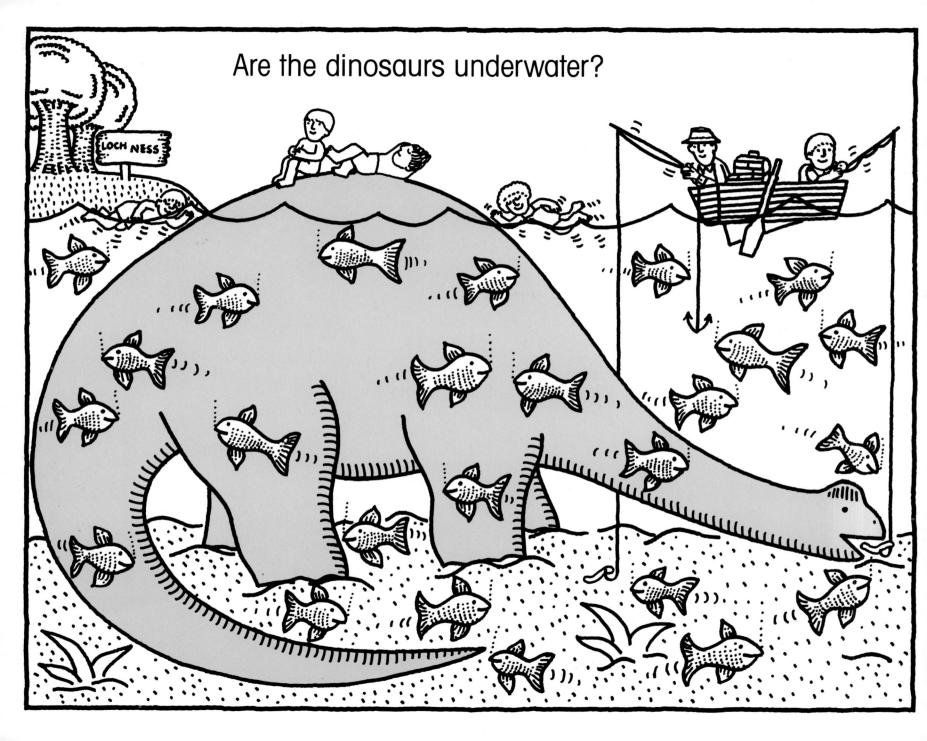

Are the dinosaurs playing hide-and-seek?

Maybe some day somebody will discover whatever happened to the dinosaurs.

Whatever happened to the Allosaurus,
the Brachiosaurus, the Camptosaurus,
the Ceratosaurus, the Cetiosaurus,
the Coelophysis, the Corythosaurus,
the Dimetrodon, the Diplodocus,
the Hypselosaurus, the Iguanodon,
the Megalosaurus, the Monoclonius,
the Ornithomimus, the Parasaurolophus,
the Plateosaurus, the Plesiosaurus,
the Protoceratops, the Scelidosaurus,
the Stegosaurus, the Trachodon,
the Triceratops, and the Tyrannosaurus?

Do you know?